Sing Along
Christmas
Carols with
Santa
MOONSTONE

Published in Moonstone
by Rupa Publications India Pvt. Ltd 2024
7/16, Ansari Road, Daryaganj
New Delhi 110002

Sales centres:
Bengaluru Chennai
Hyderabad Jaipur Kathmandu
Kolkata Mumbai Prayagraj

P-ISBN: 978-93-6156-748-3
E-ISBN: 978-93-6156-415-4

First impression 2024

10 9 8 7 6 5 4 3 2 1

Contents

AWAY IN A MANGER

Away in a manger, no crib for a bed
The little Lord Jesus laid down His sweet head
The stars in the sky looked down where He lay
The little Lord Jesus asleep on the hay
The cattle are lowing, the baby awakes
But little Lord Jesus no crying He makes
I love Thee, Lord Jesus, look down from the sky
And stay by my side until morning is nigh
Be near me, Lord Jesus, I ask Thee to stay
Close by me forever, and love me, I pray
Bless all the dear children in Thy tender care
And fit us for heaven to live with Thee there

1. A - way in a man-ger, No crib for His bed, The lit - tle Lord
2. The cat - tle are low-ing, The poor ba - by wakes, But lit - tle Lord
3. Be near me, Lord Je - sus, I ask Thee to stay Close by me for -
Je - sus Laid down His sweet head: The stars in the heav-ens Look'd
Je - sus No cry - ing He makes; I love Thee, Lord Je - sus, Look
ev - er And love me, I pray: Bless all the dear chil-dren In
down where He lay, The lit - tle Lord Je - sus A - sleep in the hay.
down from the sky, And stay by my cra-dle Till morning is nigh.
Thy ten-der care, And take us to heav-en To live with Thee there.

AULD LANG SYNE

Should auld acquaintance be forgot
And never brought to mind?
Should auld acquaintance be forgot
And days of auld lang syne?
For auld lang syne, my dear
For auld lang syne
We'll take a cup o' kindness yet
For auld lang syne
And surely ye'll be your pint-stowp!
And surely I'll be mine!
And we'll tak' a cup o' kindness yet
For auld lang syne

p
1. Should auld ac-quain-tance be for-got, And nev - er brought to mind?
2. We twa ha'e run a - boot the braes, And pu'd the gow - ans fine;
3. We twa ha'e sport - ed i' the burn, Frae morn - in' sun till dine,
4. And here's a hand, my trust - y frien', And gie's a hand o' thine;
Should auld ac-quain-tance be for - got, And days of auld lang syne?
But we've wan - der'd mon - y a wea - ry foot, Sin' auld lang syne.
But seas be-tween us braid ba'e roared Sin' auld lang syne.
We'll tak' a cup o' kind - ness yet, For auld lang syne.
9
For auld lang syne, my dear, For auld lang syne;
We'll tak' a cup o' kind - ness yet For auld lang syne.

BOARD GAME WITH SANTA!
PICK THE GIFTS HE'S LEFT FOR YOU ALONG THE WAY

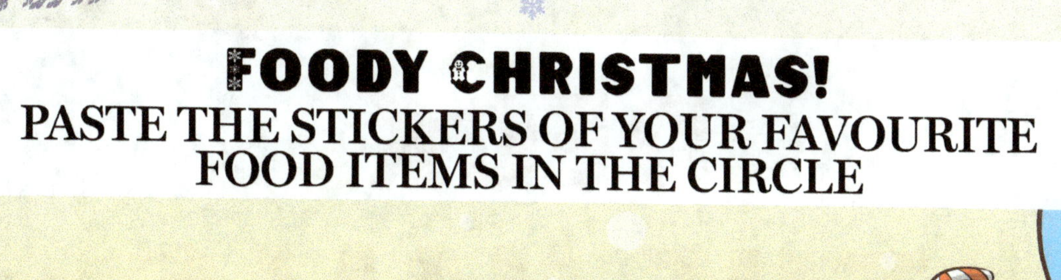

FOODY CHRISTMAS!

PASTE THE STICKERS OF YOUR FAVOURITE FOOD ITEMS IN THE CIRCLE

DECK THE HALLS

Deck the halls with boughs of holly
Fa la la la la, la la la la
Tis the season to be jolly
Fa la la la la, la la la la
Don we now our gay apparel
Fa la la, la la la, la la la
Troll the ancient Yuletide carol
Fa la la la la, la la la la
See the blazing Yule before us
Fa la la la la, la la la la
Strike the harp and join the chorus
Fa la la la la, la la la la
Follow me in merry measure
Fa la la la la, la la la la
While I tell of Yuletide treasure
Fa la la la la, la la la la

1. Deck the hall with boughs of hol - ly, Fa la la la la, la la la la.
2. See the blaz - ing Yule be - fore us, Fa la la la la, la la la la.
3. Fast a - way the old year pass - es, Fa la la la la, la la la la.
'Tis the sea - son to be jol - ly, Fa la la la la, la la la la.
Strike the harp and join the cho - rus, Fa la la la la, la la la la.
Hail the new, ye lads and lass - es, Fa la la la la, la la la la.
Don we now our gay ap-par - el; Fa la la, la la la, la la la.
Fol - low me in mer - ry mea - sure, Fa la la, la la la, la la la.
Sing we joy - ous all to-geth - er, Fa la la, la la la, la la la.
Troll the an - cient Yule - tide car - ol, Fa la la la la, la la la la.
While I tell of Yule - tide trea - sure, Fa la la la la, la la la la.
Heed - less of the wind and weath - er, Fa la la la la, la la la la.
11

WE WISH YOU A MERRY CHRISTMAS

We wish you a Merry Christmas
We wish you a Merry Christmas
We wish you a Merry Christmas
And a Happy New Year!

Good tidings we bring to you and your kin.
We wish you a merry Christmas
And a Happy New Year!

Oh, bring us some figgy pudding
Oh, bring us some figgy pudding
Oh, bring us some figgy pudding
And bring it right here!

Good tidings we bring to you and your kin.
We wish you a merry Christmas
And a Happy New Year!

mf
1, 4. We wish you a Mer-ry Christ-mas, We wish you a Mer-ry Christ-mas, We
2. Oh, bring us a fig-gy pud-ding, Oh, bring us a fig-gy pud-ding, Oh,
3. We won't go un-til we get some, We won't go un-til we get some, We

Fine
wish you a Mer-ry Christ-mas, And a hap-py New Year!
bring us a fig-gy pud-ding, and a cup of good cheer.
won't go un-til we get some, so bring it right here.
Fine

mp Good tidings to you wher-ev-er you are; Good tidings for Christmas and a happy New Year!

HELP RUDOLPH

HELP RUDOLPH COLLECT THE PRESENTS AND GET BACK TO SANTA!

WHAT'S THE DIFFERENCE?

FIND 7 DIFFERENCES IN THE TWO CHRISTMAS TREES

JINGLE BELLS

Dashing thro' the snow,
In a one-horse open sleigh,
O'er the fields we go,
Laughing all the way;
Bells on bobtail ring,
Making spirits bright;
What fun it is to ride and sing
A sleighing song tonight!

Chorus:

Jingle, bells! Jingle, bells!
Jingle all the way!
Oh! what fun it is to ride
In a one-horse open sleigh!
Jingle, bells! Jingle, bells!
Jingle all the way!
Oh! what fun it is to ride
In a one-horse open sleigh!

G
C
Swiftly
1.Dash - ing through the
snow,
In a
one horse o - pen
sleigh,

D7
G
O'er the hills we
go,
Laugh-ing all the
way!
Bells on bob tails
ring,

C
D7
G
D7
Mak-ing spi-rits
bright, What
fun it is to
laugh and sing a
sleigh-ing song to - night.
Oh!

G
D7
left hand
Jin-gle bells, Jin-gle bells, Jin-gle all the way,
Oh what fun it is to ride in a

A7
D7
G
one horse o-pen sleigh!
Jin-gle bells, Jin-gle bells, Jin-gle all the way,

D7
G
D7
G
Oh what fun it is to ride in a one horse o - pen sleigh!

HARK! THE HERALD ANGELS SING

Hark! the herald angels sing,
"Glory to the newborn King:
peace on earth, and mercy mild,
God and sinners reconciled!"
Joyful, all ye nations, rise,
join the triumph of the skies;
with th'angelic hosts proclaim,
"Christ is born in Bethlehem!"

Refrain:
Hark! the herald angels sing,
"Glory to the newborn King"

Christ, by highest heaven adored,
Christ, the everlasting Lord,
late in time behold him come,
offspring of the Virgin's womb:
veiled in flesh the Godhead see;
hail th'incarnate Deity,
pleased with us in flesh to dwell,
Jesus, our Immanuel. [Refrain]

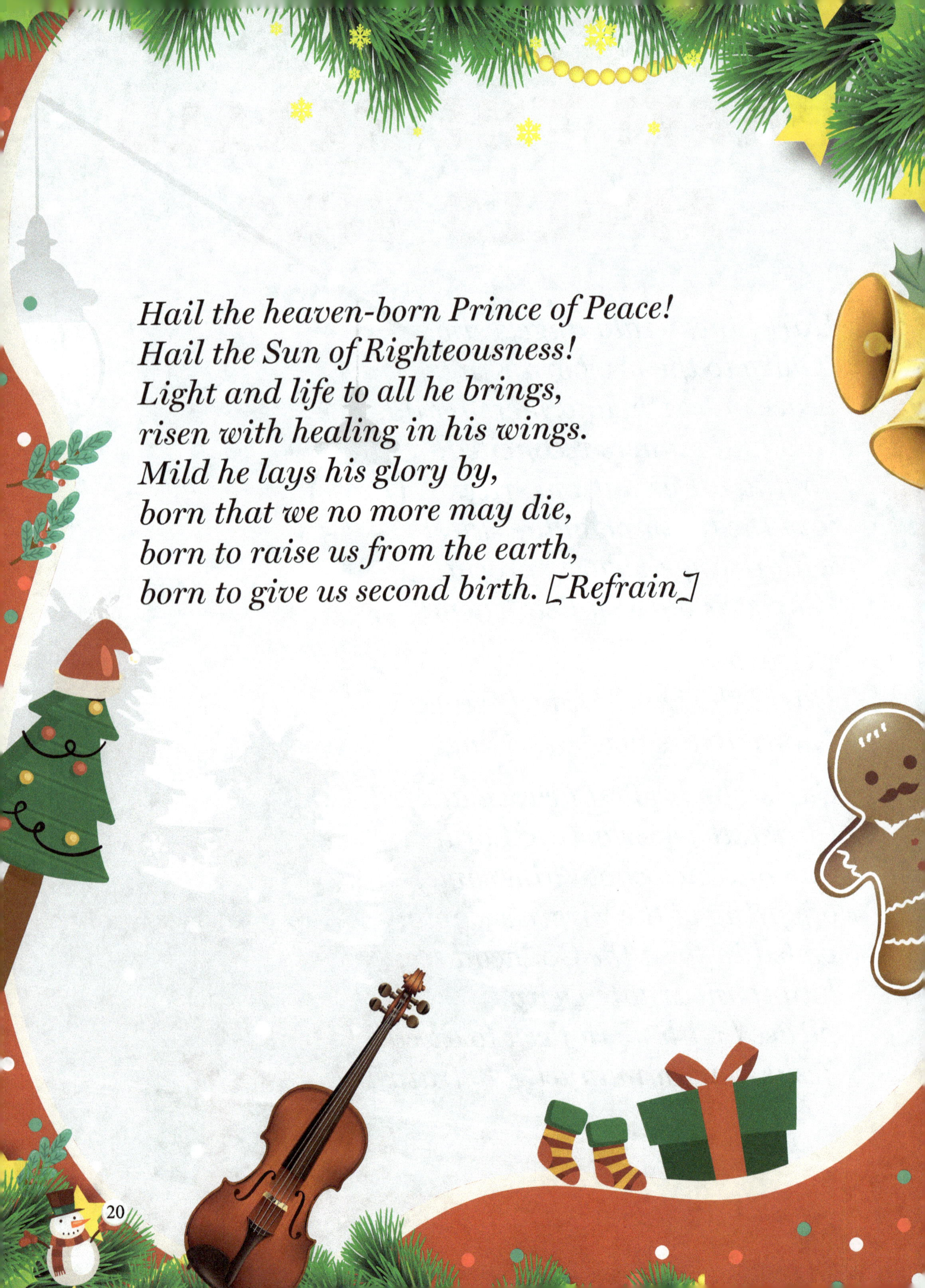

Hail the heaven-born Prince of Peace!
Hail the Sun of Righteousness!
Light and life to all he brings,
risen with healing in his wings.
Mild he lays his glory by,
born that we no more may die,
born to raise us from the earth,
born to give us second birth. [Refrain]

= 112
1. Hark! the her - ald an - gels sing, "Glo - ry to the new-born King!
2. Christ, by high - est heav'n a - dored; Christ, the ev - er - last - ing Lord;
3. Mild He lays His glo - ry by, Born that man no more may die,
Peace on earth, and mer - cy mild; God and sin - ners re - con - ciled."
Late in time be - hold Him come, Off-spring of the Vir - gin's womb.
Born to raise the sons of earth, Born to give them sec - ond birth.
Joy - ful all ye na - tions, rise; Join the tri - umph of the skies;
Veil'd in flesh the God-head see; Hail th'In - car - nate De - i - ty,
Ris'n with heal - ing in His wings, Light and life to all He brings,
With th'an - gel - ic hosts pro - claim, "Christ is born in Beth - le - hem."
Pleased as Man with man to dwell, Je - sus, our Em - man - u - el!
Hail, the Sun of Right-eous - ness! Hail, the heav'n born Prince of Peace!
Hark the her - ald an - gels sing, Glo - ry to the new-born King.

CHRISTMAS CROSSWORD

FIND THE CHRISTMAS ITEMS MISSING IN THE BLANKS

ANSWER: 1.Snowglobe 2.Deer 3.Present 4.Snowman 5.Stocking 6.Santa

AVOID THE BOMB!

JOY TO THE WORLD

Joy to the world; the Lord is come;
Let Earth receive her King;
Let ev'ry Heart prepare him room,
And Heav'n and nature sing.

Joy to the Earth, the Savior reigns,
Let men their Songs employ,
While fields and floods, rocks, hills and plains,
Repeat the sounding joy.

No more let sins and sorrows grow,
Nor thorns infest the ground;
He comes to make his blessings flow
Far as the curse is found.

He rules the world with truth and grace,
And makes the nations prove
The glories of his righteousness,
And wonders of his love.

♩=70
1. Joy to the world! the Lord is come; Let earth re -
2. Joy to the world! the Sav - ior reigns; Let men their
3. No more let sin and sor - rows grow, Nor thorns in -
4. He rules the world with truth and grace And makes the
ceive her King; Let ev - 'ry heart pre - pare Him
songs em - ploy; While fields and floods, rocks, hills and
fest the ground; He comes to make his bless - ings
na - tions prove The glo - ries of His right - eous -
room, And heav'n and na - ture sing, And heav'n and na - ture
plains Re - peat the sound - ing joy, Re - peat the sound - ing
flow Far as the curse is found, Far as the curse is
ness, And won - ders of His love, And won - ders of His
And heav'n and na - ture sing,
Re - peat the sound-ing joy,
And
Re -
sing, And heav'n, and heav'n and na - ture sing.
joy, Re - peat, re - peat the sound - ing joy.
found, Far as, far as, the curse is found.
love, And won - ders, won - ders of His love.

SILENT NIGHT

Silent night! shadowy night!
Purple dome, starry light!
Pouring splendor of centuries down,
Gold and purple, a glorious crown,
Where the manger so rude and wild
Cradles a child, a sleeping child.

Silent night! mystical night!
Kings and seers sought thy light,
Where the watch of the shepherds is kept,
Heavenly hots thro' the stillness have swept,
Clear, proclaiming a Savior born!
Singing the morn, the Christmas morn.

Holy night! heralding dawn!
Far and near breaks the morn!
Breaks the day when the Savior of men,
Bringing pardon and healing again,
"Holy harmless and undefiled,"
Cometh a child, a little child.

Tranquillo (♪ = 90)
p
1. Si - lent night! Ho - ly night! All is calm,
2. Si - lent night! Ho - ly night! Shep - herds quake
3. Si - lent night! Ho - ly night! Son of God,
all is bright. Round yon Vir - gin Moth - er and Child,
at the sight; Glo - ries stream from heav - en a - far,
love's pure light! Ra - diant beams from Thy ho - ly face,
Ho - ly In - fant, so ten - der and mild, Sleep in heav - en - ly
Heav'n - ly hosts sing Al - le - lu - ia; mf Christ, the Sav - ior is
With the dawn of re - deem - ing grace, Je - sus, Lord, at Thy
peace, Sleep in heav - en - ly peace.
born! pp Christ, the Sav - ior is born!
birth! Je - sus, Lord, at Thy birth!
27

NIGHT OF GIFTS!

DECORATE THE CHRISTMAS TREE BY DRAWING YOUR FAVOURITE ORNAMENTS AND GIFTS

MATCH THE FOLLOWING

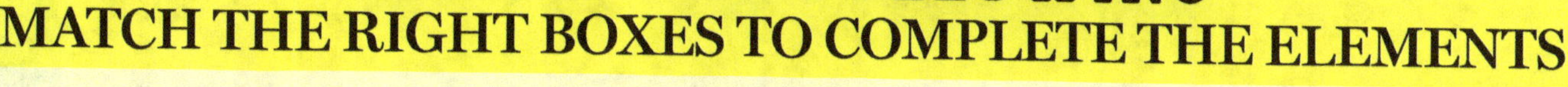

MATCH THE RIGHT BOXES TO COMPLETE THE ELEMENTS

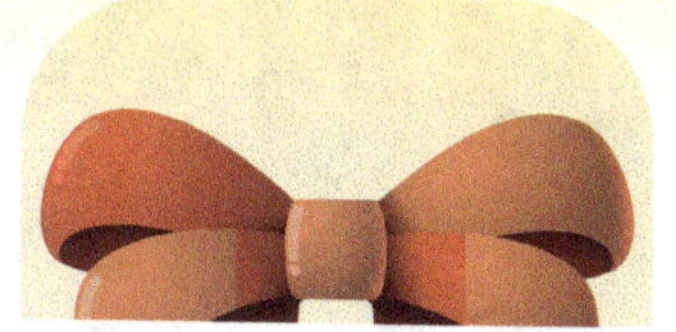   

   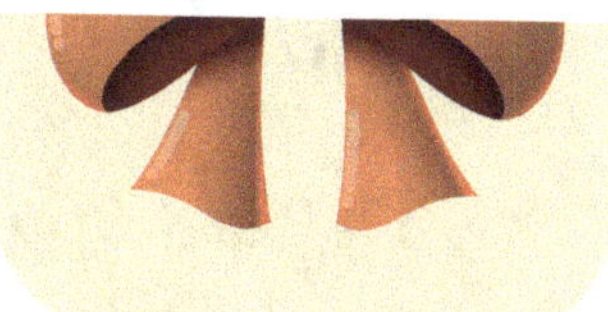

CHRISTMAS TIME IS COME AGAIN

Christmas time is come again,
Christmas pleasures bringing;
Let us join our voices now,
And Christmas songs be singing.
Years ago, one starry night,
Thus the story's given,
Angel bands o'er Bethlehem's plains,
Sang the songs of heaven.

Glory be to God on high!
Peace, good will to mortals!
Christ the Lord is born tonight,
Heav'n throws wide its portals.

Angels sang, let men reply,
And children raise their voices;
Raise the chorus loud and high,
Earth and Heav'n rejoices.
When we reach that happy place
Joyous praises bringing,
Then, before our Father's face,
We shall still be singing.

1. Christmas time is come again, Christmas plea - sures bringing; Let us join our
2. An - gels sang; let men re-ply, And chil-dren join their voi-ces; Raise the cho - rus
voi - ces now, And Christmas songs be singing. Years a - go, one starry night, Thus the sto-ry's
loud and high, Earth and heav'n re - joi-ces. When we reach that happy place, Joy-ous praises
Chorus
giv - en, An - gel bands o'er Bethlem's plains, Sang the songs of heaven. Glo-ry be to God on high!
bringing, Then, be - fore our Fa-ther's face, We shall still be singing.

www.ingramcontent.com/pod-product-compliance
Lightning Source LLC
La Vergne TN
LVHW080020110826
845148LV00019B/1171
9789361567483